Published by Hachette Partworks Ltd.
ISBN: 978-1-909766-82-2
Date of Printing: May 2014
Printed in Malaysia by
Tien Wah Press

Disney

H hachette

It was a happy day on Mount Olympus, the home of the gods of Ancient Greece. Zeus, the supreme god, and Hera, his queen, had a new baby son called Hercules.

"He's so cute!" said Zeus as the baby grabbed his finger and spun him round. "And strong too, like his dad!"

Zeus used his magical powers to make a winged horse out of clouds. "His name is Pegasus," Zeus told Hercules. "He's all yours, son."

As the other gods crowded round to admire the baby, Hades, the god of the Underworld, appeared. Fortune-tellers had told Hades that Hercules would stop him from becoming the ruler of all the gods. Hades had to get rid of that baby!

Hades ordered his two servants, Pain and Panic, to kidnap and get rid of the baby. They made him drink a magic potion so he would no longer be immortal. But before they could finish Hercules off, a human couple found him and Pain and Panic ran away.

The two henchmen turned themselves into snakes and crept back to the baby. But even though Hercules was now human, he was still incredibly strong! Pain and Panic limped off without completing their mission.

Now Hercules was mortal, he couldn't live with the other gods. He was adopted by the human couple, Alcmene and Amphitryon.

Years passed. Hercules was loved by his new family and he grew into a handsome young man. But he was often in trouble because he couldn't control his amazing strength! One night, his parents finally told him the truth about how they found him as a baby. Hercules longed to find out about his real parents.

Hercules went to the temple where, to his amazement, the giant statue of Zeus came to life!

"My boy! My little Hercules!" said Zeus.

Zeus explained the whole story to Hercules. Then he told him, "If you want to live with me on Mount Olympus, you must prove yourself a hero on Earth. Then you will be made a god again. Go to Philoctetes, the trainer of heroes."

The next day, Hercules set off on Pegasus for the island of Hydra, where Philoctetes lived.

Philoctetes, or Phil for short, was a satyr – half man, half goat. He agreed to train Hercules. In time, Hercules grew stronger, faster and braver.

One morning, Phil announced that they were going to Thebes, the greatest city in Greece.

On the way to the city, Hercules faced his first
test. He came across a beautiful young woman
struggling to escape from a centaur called Nessus.

Hercules knew that it was a hero's job to save ladies in distress, so he fought Nessus and easily defeated him.

"My name is Megara, but my friends call me Meg," said the young woman. "Who are you?"

"M-my n-name is Hercules," he shyly replied.

Although Meg looked sweet and innocent, she was really working for Hades. When Meg told her boss about meeting Hercules, he was furious – Pain and Panic were supposed to have killed him years ago!

"With him alive, I'll never defeat Zeus!" he roared. "We must act now!"

Hades sent Meg to Thebes to trick Hercules. "Help!" she cried. "There's been a rock slide. Two little boys are trapped!"

Hercules raced to the rescue and saved the boys, who were really Pain and Panic in disguise.

Suddenly, a terrifying, many-headed monster called the Hydra appeared! After an epic battle, Hercules defeated the monster – and became a hero overnight! His fan club grew and grew until soon, he was the most famous man in all of Greece.

Hades was desperate to stop Hercules becoming a god again. "He's got to have a weakness," he raged at Meg. "If you can find it, I'll let you have your freedom."

But when Meg spent the day with Hercules, she had a wonderful time. She realised that she was falling in love with him. How could she betray him now?

Bravely, Meg stood up to Hades.

"I'm not going to help you hurt Hercules," she told him. "He's honest and he's sweet!"

Hades smiled. He knew that he had discovered the young man's weakness – it was Meg!

Hades grabbed Meg and went to Hercules. "I'll let your girlfriend go if you agree to give up your strength for one day," he snarled.

"OK," said Hercules reluctantly. "But if one hair on her head is hurt, the deal's off – I get my strength back!"

Hades agreed and as they shook hands, Hercules' strength disappeared.

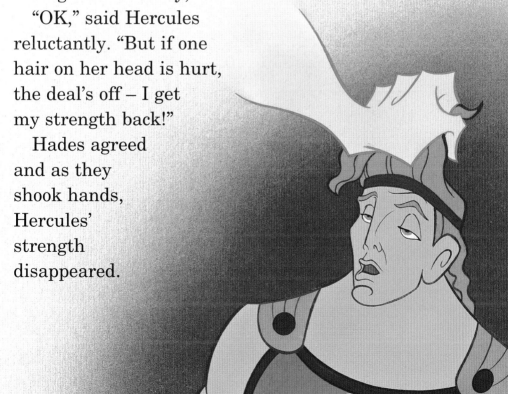

Immediately, Hades sent huge monsters called Titans to attack Mount Olympus. Then he ordered the Cyclops, a one-eyed giant, to go to Thebes and destroy Hercules.

Hercules needed help. He'd lost his strength and his hope. Meg hopped onto Pegasus and raced to find Phil. They arrived back just as Hercules was ready to give up.

Phil reminded Hercules that he still had brains, if not strength. He used a rope to trip up the Cyclops and send it plunging off a cliff. But as the monster fell, it sent a pillar crashing towards Hercules!

Meg pushed Hercules out of danger and the pillar landed on her instead. She was seriously hurt – so Hercules' strength immediately returned.

Full of grief and anger, Hercules rushed to help
his father. Soon, he had defeated the Titans and
driven them off Mount Olympus.

Hades was beaten. He fled, taking the soul of Meg with him. If Hercules wanted to save Meg, he would have to come to the Underworld and get her!

At the entrance to the Underworld stood Cerberus,
a ferocious three-headed dog. Hercules jumped on its
back and rode down to Hades' secret lair.

"Take me in Meg's place," Hercules called to Hades.

"OK, you can swim across the river and get her,"
said Hades. He was sure Hercules would die in the
River Styx before he could reach Meg.

But Hercules didn't die. The moment
he offered himself instead of Meg, his
heroic act had turned him back
into an immortal god!

Hercules flung Hades
into the bottomless pit
of the Underworld.
He would never
trouble mortals
or gods again!

"A true hero isn't measured by the size of his strength, but by the strength of his heart," said Zeus as he welcomed Hercules to Mount Olympus.

Hercules introduced Meg to his parents. "Meg is not immortal, so she can't live here," said Hercules. "Life without her would be empty, so I want to stay on Earth so we can be together."

Zeus sadly allowed Hercules to become mortal again so he could be with Meg.

But the king of the gods did one last thing to show how proud he was of his son: he created an image of Hercules out of stars, which would shine forever in honour of the young hero!